TALES THE PEOPLE TELL IN
CHINA

TALES THE PEOPLE

TELL IN
CHINA

BY ROBERT WYNDHAM

ILLUSTRATED BY
JAY YANG

CONSULTING EDITOR:
DORIS K. COBURN

JULIAN MESSNER   NEW YORK

Published by Julian Messner, a division of Simon & Schuster, Inc.,
1 West 39 Street, New York, N.Y. 10018. All rights reserved.

Copyright © 1971 by Robert Wyndham.

Printed in the United States of America
ISBN 0-671-32427-6 Cloth Trade
0-671-32428-4 MCE
Library of Congress Catalog Card No. 74-154971
Design by Marjorie Zaum K.

CONTENTS

TALES THE PEOPLE TELL IN
CHINA

DISCOVERY OF SALT

One day, in the olden times, Go Chan was working in a marshy field near the sea. He straightened his weary back, mopped his brow, and saw a wonder: a phoenix perched upon a mound of earth. "What luck!" thought he, for this fabulous bird perched only where treasure was buried. Everyone knew that.

Grasping his wooden hoe, he ran toward the mound. The phoenix flew away, and Go Chan fell upon the mound, hacking at the earth. He dug and dug, but all he turned up was clods of dirt.

"The earth itself must be the treasure," Go Chan thought. "Perhaps, at last, I've made my fortune."

He took a clod of earth home, thinking to sell it for a

great price. But soon he became troubled. People who found treasure and failed to report it to the Emperor were often put to death. Everyone knew that, too. There was nothing for him to do but to take the piece of earth to the Emperor and hope for a rich reward.

Go Chan put on his least-worn trousers and his cleanest coat. Placing the lumps of earth in a willow basket, he trudged to the palace. There he presented himself to the Emperor as a finder of treasure.

When the Emperor asked to see the treasure, Go Chan bowed low. He thrust forth the clod of earth, and then he told about the phoenix that had perched upon the mound from which the clod had come.

The Emperor leaned forward to inspect the lump of earth. His interest quickly turned to disgust. The peasant's basket contained nothing but dirt, evil-smelling dirt at that.

Angrily, the Emperor ordered his guards to seize the peasant and put him to death. Without delay the unfortunate man was beheaded.

Some time later, the Royal Cook was carrying a dish of soup to the Emperor for his dinner. It was the rainy season, when water pours from the skies and everything is damp. As he walked under a shelf in the passageway, something wet splashed into the bowl. Looking up, the cook recognized the peasant's basket, which someone had placed on the shelf. The basket was quite damp, and even as he watched, another drop splashed into the royal soup. The Royal Cook was horrified. Yet, when he inspected the soup, he saw nothing unusual in it. So the cook moved on into the royal dining hall and set the bowl before His Majesty as if nothing had happened.

The Emperor dipped his spoon into the soup. At the first taste, he looked up and smiled at the cook. "This is the same soup you have served me for many years," he remarked. "Yet today it tastes so different. What did you add to make it taste so good?"

"N—nothing, Your Majesty," the cook replied. But with the Emperor's eyes upon him, he decided to tell the truth. "As I was carrying the soup to you, a few drops of moisture fell into it," he confessed.

"Moisture? From what?" the Emperor demanded.

The cook turned pale. "From the clod of earth that peasant brought to you some weeks ago, Your Majesty. Somehow, someone put the basket on the kitchen shelf...and..." He was too terrified to continue.

"Extraordinary," murmured the Emperor. Then, remembering the story of the phoenix, he began to wonder if the clod of earth might be a treasure after all. He ordered the cook to fetch the basket so that he could inspect the contents once more.

Drip, drip—plop! Dampness from the clod of earth dripped steadily through the willow basket. His Majesty held out his hand, caught a drop, and tasted it. The flavor pleased him. Where the drips had fallen on the floor and dried, the Emperor saw patches of white crystals.

Immediately, men were sent to the mound to dig. The earth they brought back was soaked with water, the drippings were caught and dried in the sun until they became crystals of salt. These were used to flavor the food in the Imperial Kitchen.

Soon, other salt mounds and marshes were discovered in the kingdom. As the quantity of salt increased, the Emperor sold the salt to the nobles, then to the people. His treasure rooms bulged with the salt-money.

Alas, nothing could be done to reward the old peasant, Go Chan. However, his son was brought to the court and put in charge of the Imperial Salt Mounds. The youth grew rich and powerful and rose to higher and higher positions in government office. So Go Chan, honored through his son, at last rested peacefully among his ancestors.

THE WISE MAN'S PILLOW

Long ago in old Cathay, a farm youth trudged along a dusty road. Soon he overtook an elderly man, who was dressed in the fine, long robe of a priest and was carrying a traveling bag tucked under his arm.

"Honorable sir," the youth addressed him. "Allow me to walk beside you. I can see by your robe that you are a man of learning. Perhaps you will give me a willow twig of wisdom to chew on, for I am most unhappy."

"How so?" the old priest asked as they fell into step. "You are young and in fine health. Your eyes do not have the look of one haunted by evil spirits."

"Nevertheless, I am a miserable wretch," the youth said. "Look at my clothes! They are the rough, short garments of a farmer, not the fine, long robes of a man with a high station in life."

"Your clothes are made for hard wear and are useful for your work. They are not rags to freeze in," the old scholar answered.

But the youth sighed and shook his head.

When the two came to an inn, the old gentleman beckoned to the youth to follow him inside. There the innkeeper was steaming a pot of rice, and the priest invited his young companion to share a bowl with him.

Placing his traveling bag on a bench, he sat down beside it. "While we wait," he said to his young guest, "tell me why you are not content with your life."

"Ah, there are many reasons, honorable sir," the youth replied. "I work from dawn to dusk. There is no time for learning or for pleasure. Actually, I am ambitious. I want to rise in the world. I would like to be a general, famous for winning great battles, or a rich man with a splendid house. I would like to study and become a great man in the court of the Emperor."

The scholar nodded.

"If I rose from a poor farm laborer to a high position, I   *15* could bring wealth and honor to my family," the youth said dreamily.

"True, true," the scholar murmured in a gentle, soothing voice.

The youth suddenly became so sleepy that he could scarcely keep his eyes open. The scholar sat nodding and smiling. Then he reached inside his traveling bag and brought out a long, round pillow. It was made of porcelain and shaped like a tube open at both ends.

"Stretch out on this bench, my friend," he said softly. "Lay your head on this pillow, and all your dreams may come true."

As the young farmer was about to put his head on the pillow, he noticed that one of the openings was very large. Inside, it was very bright. It looked so inviting that he climbed in—and found that he was in his own home. Yet now, it was no longer a humble peasant cottage, but a richly furnished house. On the walls were silk hangings. The tables were decorated with mother-of-pearl, and on them stood objects of precious jade. The library was filled with great books written on fine scrolls.

For several years, he studied the books of the master

Kung. He passed his examinations with high honors, and he was made a magistrate. Soon after, the youth married the daughter of an important family. And, in a few years, he rose to the trusted position of Prime Minister to the Emperor.

As he gained power, other advisors to the Emperor became jealous of his importance, and they plotted against him. They accused him of treason and of stealing from the royal treasury.

The Emperor, believing these lies, sentenced his Prime Minister to death. Along with common criminals, he was taken to the place of execution. There he was made to kneel. The executioner approached and raised his great sword. The Prime Minister was so terrified that he did not feel the terrible blow as the sword came down . . .

In the instant that he should have died, the farm youth opened his eyes to find himself at the inn. The wise old scholar was seated at the table, ready to eat. The innkeeper was heaping steamed rice into his bowl.

The dazed youth staggered to the table to join the priest. The two ate in silence. When his bowl was empty, the youth stood up. He bowed deeply, saying, "Now I know how a man can rise to great position in the world, and how easily he can be cut down. I thank you for your magic pillow, and for the lesson it taught me."

With another deep bow, the young man left the inn and returned to his work.

THE MARVELOUS PEAR SEED

Sha-shih Ya-po was a poor man. Sometimes, driven by hunger, he stole a roll. Driven by need, he sometimes stole a piece of cloth. One day, thinking that no one would see him, Sha-shih Ya-po stole a pear.

He had not yet finished eating it when the fruit vendor pointed him out to the police. Sha-shih Ya-po managed to hide the core of the pear inside his shirt before the police hauled him off to jail. There the poor thief finished eating the pear core, all but one small brown seed. This he wrapped carefully in a bit of paper which he stuffed inside his sash. Now and then he took the paper out, unwrapped the little seed and gazed upon it, remembering the tasty pear from which it had come.

20

Days passed and months, too. Still, Sha-shih Ya-po had not been brought to trial. He began to wonder if he would ever get out of his dank prison cell. And then, as he gazed at his little pear seed, an idea took shape in his mind.

"Guard! Guard!" he shouted. "I want to see the Emperor!"

"Why do *you* want to see the Emperor?" the astonished guard asked.

"I have a rare gift for him," Sha-shih Ya-po answered. "Take me to the palace at once."

When the Emperor saw a ragged thief before him, he asked, "What sort of gift can you possibly have for me?"

"This, Your Majesty," said the thief, pulling out the paper

with the pear seed wrapped in it.

The Emperor unwrapped the paper. "It is nothing but an ordinary pear seed," he exclaimed.

"Ah," sighed the thief. "That is not an ordinary pear seed at all. Your Majesty, if you will but plant it, it will grow into a marvelous tree, which will bear pears of pure gold."

"If that is so," the Emperor asked, "why did you not plant the seed yourself?"

"Alas," said the thief, "for me the tree would bear only ordinary pears. It will not bear golden fruit unless it is planted by a person who has never stolen anything in his life, or cheated anyone either. That is why I have brought this seed to you, Your Majesty. Surely you have never stolen anything in your life, or cheated anyone."

The Emperor frowned. He knew he could not plant the seed and expect golden pears from it either. As a little boy, he had stolen sweets from his nurse. Later, well, there were other things. And most recently, there was the estate he had taken from the nobleman he had beheaded for some reason or other. No, he could not risk planting the pear seed. The Emperor shook his head.

"Let your Prime Minister plant it then," Sha-shih Ya-po urged.

22

"No, no, I could not!" the Prime Minister exclaimed. "There might be some small thing in my past life—long ago, of course—that I have forgotten." Not to mention the bribes he accepted, the gifts he demanded, the court records he changed to improve his own fortunes. The Prime Minister's eyes bulged from worry.

"Well, what about the commander of the Royal Army?" the thief suggested, noting that this worthy person was in the audience hall.

"No, no!" The commander stepped back in alarm. He remembered that there were certain officers he had cheated of a promotion because others had been able to pay for higher rank. Then there was that horse he had kept for himself, when it should have gone into the royal stables. No, the commander could not risk planting the remarkable pear seed.

"What about your Chief Magistrate, then?" the thief suggested. "Surely *he* has nothing but clean wind in his sleeves."

However, even the Chief Magistrate could not plant the seed, for he did not always decide the cases before him honestly.

"What about the Chief Warden of the Royal Prisons?" the thief prodded.

The Chief Warden backed away from the idea. *He* 23

accepted money from prisoners for better treatment. Frequently, many strings of cash were given to him to lighten a prisoner's punishment.

So it went, down to the lowest page attending His Majesty. No one would plant the seed that would produce golden pears. Each one found that he could not do it, for his own conscience was not clear.

Sha-shih Ya-po said, "Everyone of you has admitted that he lies, steals, and cheats, yet *you* do not have to go to prison for it. I, poor Sha-shih Ya-po, because I stole a pear when I was hungry, I have been cast into prison and forgotten. Your Majesty, is this justice?"

The Emperor looked at the poor man before him and shook his head. "Go, Sha-shih Ya-po," he said. "You are a free man."

THE YOUNG HEAD
OF THE CHENG FAMILY

In the Cheng family, there were a father, three sons, and two young daughters-in-law. Plum Blossom and Peony were brides of the elder brothers, and they had but recently been brought into the household. Both girls came from a village a few miles beyond the Cheng farm, and they both grew homesick frequently. Since they had no mother-in-law living, they had to ask their father-in-law for permission to visit their parents. This became quite a bother to the old man.

The next time they begged to visit their mothers, he said, "You may go, but only on one condition. When you return, you must bring me things I want. You, Plum Blossom, must bring me some fire wrapped in paper. And you, Peony, must bring me some wind on a paper. If you fail to get these things for me, you are never to come back here."

Old Cheng thought that the girls would not accept these conditions for their visit. But they were so eager to get away, they would have promised him anything.

It was a long, hot walk to their native village. After a while, they sat down to rest by the roadside. When they began to think of their promises to their father-in-law, some of their happiness drained away. Before long, both girls were weeping noisily.

As they sat there rocking and crying, a young girl rode out of a field on the back of a big water buffalo. "Are you in trouble?" she asked.

"*Ai-yee, ai-yee!*" wailed the girls, and they told her of the promises they had made to their father-in-law.

Instead of grieving with them, the girl, whose name was Precious Jade, laughed. "Dry your tears!" she said. "Come home with me. I will show you how to bring your father-in-law exactly what he wants. And then you can go and have a happy visit with your mothers."

When they reached her father's house, Precious Jade gave Plum Blossom a paper lantern. "When you light the candle inside this lantern, your father-in-law will have his

fire wrapped in paper," she said. To Peony, she gave a paper fan. "Wave the fan. There is some wind on paper!" she exclaimed.

The two young wives thanked Precious Jade again and again. Then they fairly flew to the homes of their mothers.　27

There, they had a glorious visit with their little sisters and brothers, and they returned to their father-in-law happily.

"What!" he shouted. "You have dared to come back without the things I commanded you to bring me?"

"Oh, no, Most Honorable Father-in-Law!" exclaimed the young wives. "Here are the things you wanted."

The old man was astonished when he saw the lantern and the fan. He wondered how his flighty young daughters-in-law could suddenly have become so clever. He did not have to wonder long, because the girls soon told him about Precious Jade.

"What a remarkable young person!" he thought, stroking his wispy gray beard. "I should like to have her in the family."

At once, Old Cheng engaged the services of a go-between. Before long, a marriage was arranged, and Cheng's youngest son married Precious Jade.

When the wedding festivities were over, Old Cheng made Precious Jade the female head of the household. She was to take charge of everything.

Before the young sons returned to their work in the fields, they went to Precious Jade for instructions, as their father had ordered. She told them never to go to or from the fields empty-handed. When they went to the fields, they were to carry tools or seed or fertilizers. When they returned, they were to bring bundles of sticks for firewood. Her instructions were sensible, and the men followed them faithfully. So the sons kept the farm in fine condition. They gathered so much fuel that it was not necessary to buy even one stick of firewood that whole winter.

In the spring, Precious Jade told the men to gather up all the stones in the field and to heap them in the courtyard near the house.

One day, Yu Kai, a man who went about the countryside to buy precious stones, passed the great pile of stones in the Chengs' yard. He had no more than glanced at the heap when he saw a large piece of precious green jade. In order to get a bargain, Yu Kai pretended that he wanted the stones to build a bridge. He offered to buy the whole heap for a trifling sum. But Precious Jade became suspicious of the stranger. Instead of agreeing to his price, she asked an unreasonably large sum for the pile. She refused to consider anything less. To her surprise, the stranger agreed to the high price she had set. He told Precious Jade he would return in two days to remove the stones and bring her the money.

When the stranger left, Precious Jade looked thoughtfully at the pile of stones. They appeared to be quite ordinary, and yet she realized that there must be something of great value in them. Could it be that there was a gem in that heap of rocks?

The next day, Precious Jade sent her father-in-law to invite Yu Kai to a feast. She advised the men of her household to serve the best wine to their guest. Before dinner, she asked her father-in-law to bring the conversation around to precious stones, and to ask their guest just how one could recognize a gem among ordinary rocks.

Everything was done as she instructed. And their guest proved himself to be very fond of good wine. After the feast the ladies left the room, and the men continued drinking and talking. Precious Jade hid behind a screen. When their guest had gotten pleasantly tipsy, his tongue loosened. In no time at all, the girl learned what she needed to know.

As soon as it was light Precious Jade hastened to the rock pile. She found the piece of jade and removed it from the heap.

When Yu Kai came to collect his pile of rocks, he saw that the value had departed from his purchase. He went to see Precious Jade again. This time, she bargained so shrewdly that she was able to get from him not only the original high price for the rock pile, but an additional sum for the jade stone.

Before this, the Cheng family had been well-off. Now they were wealthy. They built a splendid ancestral hall, and over the entrance Precious Jade had inscribed the words *No Sorrow*.

One day, a mandarin passed that way and noticed the remarkable inscription. He ordered his sedan chair set down before the Cheng door, and he sent for the head of the family.

When Precious Jade appeared, he was astonished. "Yours is a most unusual family," he declared. "Never before have I seen one without sorrow. Nor have I ever seen a family with such a young head. You are much too bold. Therefore, I will make you pay a fine. You must weave for me a piece of cloth as long as this road."

Precious Jade put her hands together and bowed respectfully before the great man. "I will begin weaving the moment Your Excellency tells me exactly how long this road is," she told him.

The mandarin gave her a long hard look. "I will also fine you as much oil as there is water in the Eastern Sea," he told her.

Again Precious Jade bowed respectfully. "Excellency, if you will measure the sea and tell me exactly how much water it contains, I will begin at once to press the oil from my beans."

"Indeed!" gasped the mandarin. "Since you are so clever,

perhaps you will tell me what I am thinking. If you do, I will give you no more fines. In my hand is my pet quail. Tell me, do I mean to hold on to it or to set it free?"

"Your Excellency," Precious Jade said calmly, "I am an ordinary girl, and you are a mandarin, a great magistrate. If, sir, you know no more of these matters than I do, you have no right to fine me at all. Observe that I stand with one foot on one side of the threshold and the other foot on the other side. Tell me, do I mean to go into the house or to come out of it? If you cannot guess my riddle—you who are so great and wise—you should not ask me to guess yours."

The mandarin glared at the clever young head of the Cheng family. His eyes sparkled, and he laughed. "I can now understand the inscription above your doorway," he said. "The spirits of sorrow would not dare to pass over your threshold, for then they would have *you* to deal with!" Still laughing, he ordered his bearers to pick up his sedan chair and move on. And the Cheng family continued to prosper.

GIFT OF THE UNICORN

In ancient times, Ki-lin, the fabulous unicorn, appeared occasionally before the emperors. They said the creature was as large as a deer, but it had hoofs like a horse. It had a single horn in the center of its noble head. Its voice was beautiful and as haunting as a monastery bell. And it was so good and gentle that it walked with the greatest care, lest it step upon some living creature. The Ki-lin could neither be captured nor injured by any man. And it appeared only to those emperors who had wisdom and virtue.

When the Middle Kingdom fell into evil ways, and one state warred with another, and kings fought with kings, the unicorn was seen no more. He was seen by no one until the sixth century B.C.

At that time, there lived a woman in the town of Chufu, in the state of Lu, at the base of the sacred mountain Tai Shan. This woman was good and dutiful and truly exceptional. Her one grief was that she had given her husband no son. To be without a son was a great sorrow. If a family had no son, who would worship before the ancestral tablets? With no one to worship, there could be no life after death for the ancestors.

This good woman sorrowed and prayed and begged heaven to take pity upon her and give her a son. Yet no son was born to her.

One day, she decided to make a pilgrimage to a distant temple on the sacred Tai Shan. This temple was thought to be especially holy. There, she planned to appeal to the gods one last time.

As she trudged up the mountain toward the lonely temple, she unknowingly stepped into the secret footprint of the Ki-lin, the gentle unicorn.

At once, the marvelous creature appeared before her, knelt, and dropped a piece of precious jade at her feet. The woman picked up the jade and found these words carved upon the jewel:

"Thy son shall be a ruler without a throne."

When the woman looked up, the unicorn had vanished.   *35*

But the jade was still in her hand, and she knew that a miracle had taken place.

In time, a son was born to this good woman. He was named Kung Fu Tzu, Confucius. From his earliest days, he showed unusual wisdom, and later, he became a great teacher. Accompanied by his pupils, he traveled from town to town. All over the land, the people studied and lived by his wise sayings. His influence was as powerful as that of the emperors. Indeed, he ruled without a throne.

THE MAN WHO
STOLE A ROPE

As the constable led him into the marketplace, Jen Ho-Ho staggered under the weight of the huge wooden *cangue*, which was fastened around his neck.

"Do not move from this spot," the constable ordered. "I will come for you when the sun sets and take you back to jail."

"I will probably be dead by then," Jen Ho-Ho told him. "With this wide collar, I can neither feed myself nor drink. My fingers cannot reach my mouth. Surely I shall starve."

"Beg, then," the constable advised. "Someone may take pity on you and put some food in your mouth."

One long hour passed, then another and another. Street boys danced around Jen Ho-Ho, jeering. The drum in the clock tower boomed out the passing hours. Just before the sun set, the prisoner heard a friendly voice.

"Jen Ho-Ho, what have you been doing to deserve punishment such as this?" his neighbor, Sung Tao, asked him.

"Oh, it was scarcely anything," Jen Ho-Ho replied. "I only picked up a rope."

"And you are being punished so severely for merely picking up a rope?" his friend exclaimed.

"*Ah-hee,*" Jen Ho-Ho sighed, "there was a young ox tied to the other end."

THE BORROWING OF
100,000 ARROWS

Long ago, China was divided into small kingdoms, which were frequently at war with one another. Early in the third century, the kingdoms of Shu and Wu united in a fight against the most powerful of the three, the kingdom of Wei. All three kingdoms had military camps on the Yangtze River, with fleets of little warships that engaged in naval battles.

The commander of the powerful Wei kingdom was Tsao Ts'ao whose camp was on the north bank of the Yangtze.

The leader of Wu, the smallest and weakest kingdom, was K'ung-ming, a clever and courageous general. The commander-in-chief was Chou Yu of Shu kingdom. Although the two countries were allies, the two leaders were rivals. Chou

Yu was so jealous of K'ung-ming that he constantly plotted to get rid of his rival, but to do it in such a way that no blame would fall on him.

In order to find out what was going on in K'ung-ming's camp, Chou Yu kept the gossipy go-between, Lu Su, running back and forth between the two camps. But the clever K'ung-ming guessed the purpose of the go-between's visits, and he resolved to outsmart Chou Yu at the first opportunity.

One day, all the officers were summoned to the main tent of Chou Yu, the commander-in-chief. When K'ung-ming arrived, Chou Yu said, "I am going to fight a battle with the enemy on the river. What weapons would be best for this?"

"On the great river, arrows are the best," K'ung-ming replied.

"Your opinion and mine agree," Chou Yu said. "But at the moment, we are short of arrows. I wish you would undertake to supply about a hundred thousand arrows for this naval battle. As this is for the national good of both our countries, I hope you will not refuse my request."

K'ung-ming bowed politely. "Whatever task the commander-in-chief sets before me, I will certainly try to perform. By what date do you require the hundred thousand arrows?"

"Could you have them ready in ten days?"

"The enemy is close by," K'ung-ming said. "Ten days may be too late."

"In how many days do you think the arrows could be ready?" Chou Yu asked.

"Let me have three days," K'ung-ming told him. "Then send for your hundred thousand arrows."

"This is no joking matter," Chou Yu said.

"Would I dare joke with the commander-in-chief?" K'ung-ming asked. "Give me a direct military order to fulfill this task, and if I have not done so in three days, I will take my punishment."

Chou Yu could scarcely hide his delight. "I shall have to congratulate you most heartily when this has been accomplished," he said.

Again K'ung-ming bowed. "On the third day from tomorrow, send your boats to my camp on the river, to carry away the arrows." With this K'ung-ming took his leave.

Lu Su turned to the commander-in-chief. "Do you think he is up to some trickery?" he asked.

Chou Yu smiled. "I think he has signed his death warrant. As you saw and heard, I did not urge him to take on this task. Yet he asked me to issue a formal order to him, with all of my officers witnessing it. He cannot possibly escape me. However, just to make certain he will not succeed, I will order the arrow-makers to delay as much as possible. And then, when K'ung-ming has to pay the penalty, who can say a word against me? I will be obliged to do my military duty. Now, go and see what K'ung-ming is about, and keep me informed."

When Lu Su sidled into K'ung-ming's tent, he felt rather sorry for the courageous general of the Wu forces.

K'ung-ming did not seem surprised to see the go-between. "The commander does not have my welfare at heart," he said. "How can I get one hundred thousand arrows? You will have to help me."

Lu Su was taken aback. "You brought this on yourself," he reminded K'ung-ming. "Besides, how can I help you?"

"The admirals of the Shu fleet are your friends and your countrymen. You can get them to lend me twenty fast, light ships," K'ung-ming said. "For each ship, I want a crew of thirty men. I want bundles of straw stacked on the decks, and straw bundles lashed to the sides of each boat. I have good use for all this."

Lu Su hurried off to carry out K'ung-ming's strange request.

The ships, crews, and bundles of straw were assembled and placed at K'ung-ming's command. The general did nothing **43** with them on the first day, nor on the second. Toward evening of the third day, he sent a message asking Lu Su to come to his boat.

"Why have you sent for me?" Lu Su asked.

"I want you to go with me to get the arrows," K'ung-ming replied.

"Where are we going?"

"You shall see. For now, make yourself comfortable with me here in my cabin," K'ung-ming invited.

While the two men sat drinking wine, the twenty ships were joined together by a long rope. The sailors were ordered to row the ships over to the north bank of the river. The night was foggy, and the mist was so dense that one man at the oars could scarcely see another. In spite of the fog, K'ung-ming urged the boats forward, until they reached Tsao Ts'ao's naval base. Then, orders were given to place the boats in a line, with all their prows pointing to the west.

This done, the crews were sent below decks, and another order was given. Suddenly drums pounded and wild yells burst from the sailors.

Lu Su, who by now realized where the twenty ships were, jumped up in alarm. "What shall we do if the enemy attacks us?" he shouted above the din.

44 K'ung-ming smiled and took another sip from his cup of

wine. "I do not think Tsao Ts'ao's fleet will venture out in this fog. Drink, and let us be happy. We will return to our own base when the fog lifts."

In the enemy camp, as soon as the uproar on the river was heard, Tsao Ts'ao rushed out to peer down at the ghostlike ships. The vessels seemed unusually wide, and the decks appeared to be thick with fighting men.

"Sailing up in a fog like this means that they have prepared an ambush," Tsao Ts'ao told his aides. "We shall not sail out to fight them. Instead, get all our archers up onto the river-bank and have them shoot arrows down at these invaders."

Soon thousands of arrows rained down onto the straw bundles on the decks and into those lashed to the sides of the invading ships.

On board the ships, the pounding of drums and the shouting continued. Then the ships' prows were turned. Now they pointed to the east, with their opposite sides exposed to the enemy archers.

As the sun rose and the fog began to lift, K'ung-ming signaled for the noise to cease. His fleet turned southward, toward home base. As they sailed away, the crews began a mocking shout, "Thank you, Tsao Ts'ao, for all the arrows!"

Too late, the commander of the Wei saw that he had

been tricked.

On the way downriver, K'ung-ming said to his companion, "Each boat must have at least five or six thousand arrows stuck into its bundles of straw. Without engaging the services of a single arrow-maker, we have more than one hundred thousand arrows—borrowed from Tsao Ts'ao. Tomorrow, Chou Yu can shoot them all back at him."

"Your cleverness is more than human," Lu Su declared. "How did you know there would be a thick fog last night?"

"One cannot be a leader without knowing something of the workings of heaven and the ways of earth—and the behavior of men," K'ung-ming said. "Weather signs told me three days ago that there would be a fog last night, and so I set the three-day limit for my task."

When the ships arrived at K'ung-ming's camp, a company of men were on the riverbank. K'ung-ming ordered the men to come aboard, collect the arrows, and bear them to the tent of their commander-in-chief. Lu Su went along to report how the deed had been accomplished.

Chou Yu heard Lu Su's report with growing amazement. "Clearly," he mused, "K'ung-ming has carried out his orders superbly. He will have to be congratulated, not executed." Chou Yu sighed.

THE MAN WHO
SOLD A GHOST

One night, young Tsung Ting-po was out walking when he thought he saw someone drifting over the road. "Who are you?" Ting-po called out.

"A ghost," the other replied. "Who are you?"

"I am also a ghost," Ting-po quickly declared, for he knew ghosts played tricks on live humans.

The ghost asked where he was going, and Ting-po told him he was on the way to the market at the town of Yuan. "I want to go there too," the ghost said.

They set off together. After traveling a number of *li*, the ghost said it was foolish for both of them to walk when they

48

could take turns carrying each other.

"An excellent idea," Ting-po agreed.

Thereupon, the ghost had Ting-po get up on his back and carried him for several *li*. "You are extremely heavy," the ghost remarked. "Could it be that you are not a ghost?"

"I have died only recently," Ting-po explained. "That is why I am still heavy. Anyway, it is now my turn to carry you."

Ting-po carried the ghost easily, for it had no weight at all. Thus they carried one another by turns, with the ghost complaining each time about his companion's extraordinary weight. "I am newly dead," Ting-po reminded the ghost. Then he added, "Along with still being heavy, there are many things I do not yet know. For instance, what should a ghost fear the most?"

"Human saliva," the ghost answered promptly. "When we are touched by it, we cannot play tricks on people."

They came to a stream, and Ting-po allowed the ghost to cross to the other side first. Then Ting-po stepped into the water and swish-swashed across.

"Why did you make that sound?" the ghost demanded.

"I have been telling you," Ting-po said. "I am a new ghost. I am not used to getting through water properly." But he knew the ghost was becoming more and more suspicious of him. *49*

Ting-po grasped the ghost, swung him over his shoulder, and held him tight.

"Let me go!" the ghost shouted, and he struggled to free himself. "Now I know you are not a ghost," he declared. Ting-po gripped him all the more tightly.

When they reached the center of town, the ghost made himself very thin and slid off Ting-po's shoulder. Then he changed himself into a large goat, ready to butt his human companion.

Instantly, Ting-po spat on the goat—once, and again for good measure, so it could not change itself into anything else. A man came along and offered a price for the goat, and Ting-po sold it for fifteen hundred *cash*.

Since that day, when the time is just right in China, one man will remind another that Tsung Ting-po sold a *ghost* for fifteen hundred *cash*.

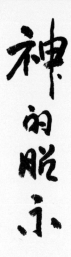

A WARNING FROM THE GODS

During the Ming Dynasty, the city of Ta-yeh, on the Yangtze River, in the province of Hupei, was noted for its wickedness. Yet in the midst of its wicked and heedless people, there lived a good woman named Niang-tzu. This woman ate no meat, she never killed a living creature, and she never took anything that did not belong to her. She never lied, and she did not gossip, nor was she ever guilty of an unkind deed.

One night she had a dream, a vision, in which she saw the city of Ta-yeh and the whole region around it flooded by deep water. Nothing had been spared. Everything had been destroyed. Niang-tzu woke up trembling, and heard a voice which said that there would be a sign from the gods before the floods came. "When the stone lions before the *yamen* of the mandarin weep tears of blood, then destruction will be near at hand."

As soon as it was light, the good Niang-tzu hurried out into the streets of the city to warn everyone of the coming disaster. Day after day, she walked the streets, telling of the calamity. Everyone laughed at her. Some said that she was mad. Besides, no tears of blood had fallen from the eyes of the stone lions at the gate of the mandarin's *yamen*.

One day, the butcher, who was fond of jokes, took some

pig blood and smeared it on the eyes of the stone lions.

When Niang-tzu saw the blood-stained eyes, she ran through the city, crying out her warning. But this was met by gales of laughter and cruel jests and jeering. The good woman ran from the doomed city, and she did not stop until she could run no more.

Soon after she left the city gates, the sky grew dark. Thunder roared. A mighty earthquake shook the land, and the city of Ta-yeh sank into a hollow. Before anyone could escape, the waters of the Yangtze River swirled into this hollow and covered the city and the villages around it.

Only one spot of ground remained above water. This was the place where the good Niang-tzu had stopped to rest. To this day, the island, called Niang-tzu in her honor, rises out of the center of the great Liang-ti Lake. In the shelter of Niang-tzu Island, boats anchor at night. When storms sweep over the lake, ships rush to take shelter in the island's coves.

On sunny days, when the waters of the lake are clear and still, people say that they can see traces of the buried city of Ta-yeh. Now and then, a fisherman hauls in his nets and finds some household utensil from olden times there among the fish.

LEGEND OF HOW ANTS CAME TO EARTH

Pan Tzu had a wife who nagged him day and night because he never earned enough money to make her happy. At last, when Pan Tzu could stand her nagging no longer, he left their home and their village to find a job elsewhere. He wandered from place to place, but could find no work. He missed his little son, and even his nagging wife. Finally he grew so homesick that he returned to his native village.

When Pan Tzu came to his house, he was afraid to enter. He knew his wife would scold him because, as usual, he had no money. So he lingered outside.

While he hid in the shadows, he heard his wife tell their son about the food she had purchased at the market that day. *55*

He listened to their talk and to the sounds she made as she put the food away in the cupboard.

After a while, Pan Tzu worked up enough courage to enter the house. His wife did not greet him. Instead, she gave him a sharp look and asked him why he had bothered to come back home. "I can see you are as empty-handed as when you went away," she shouted. "If it weren't for the kindness of my uncles, our little son and I would have starved."

"Yes, yes, I know," Pan Tzu broke in hastily. And then, a clever idea sprang into his mind. "You see, while I was away, I discovered that I have a remarkable sense of smell. In fact, it is quite magical. I decided to return home and put it to use somehow."

"Oh, you did!" she sneered. "Then put it to use right now and tell me what there is to eat in this house."

Pan Tzu sniffed the air. "A chicken," he told her, "ready to be cooked."

His wife was surprised, but she was not convinced. "What else does your newly found gift tell you?" she asked.

Pan Tzu sniffed to the left and to the right. "My dear wife, there is pork near that chicken."

Now, his wife was truly amazed, but still not entirely convinced. "What else can your magic sense of smell tell you?"

Pan Tzu sniffed right and left. "You have fish . . ." He sniffed again. "Ah, yes! It is carp. And you have several vegetables . . . Oh . . . there is even some delicious bean curd in that cupboard."

His wife was so impressed by this proof of his remarkable sense of smell that she invited him to join the family at supper.

Next day, she went to the village to tell her neighbors about the talent her husband had for smelling out anything. The gossip spread from village to village. Each time the story was repeated, Pan Tzu's special talent grew greater. It was said he could find anything, anywhere, just by sniffing the air. Soon the Emperor heard about this unusual man, and he ordered him to appear at the winter palace.

When the terrified Pan Tzu arrived, he fell to his knees and kowtowed to the Emperor, knocking his head nine times upon the marble floor.

"I have lost a valuable jade seal," the Emperor said. "Use your supernatural sense of smell to find it, and you may choose your reward."

Pan Tzu, who had been enjoying his local fame, now deeply regretted the lie he had told his wife. It had seemed harmless enough. Now it had brought him to this. What would the Emperor do when he discovered that Pan Tzu had no

extraordinary power whatever!

The poor fellow began to whimper and moan to himself. "I can feel the Emperor's *sharp sword* upon my neck. *Ai! There is no hope for me!*" Over and over, he mumbled these words as he shuffled about the room, sniffing the air.

The nobles of the Emperor's court thought that Pan Tzu had gone into the trance which usually comes before a man uses his supernatural powers. While listening to him, two mandarins turned pale. To one, *sharp sword* sounded like *Sha-Su*, which was his name. To the other, the words *Ai! there is no hope for me!* sounded exactly like his name, *Ai Ti Ho*.

"We are done for," one whispered to the other, "unless we can get this magician to listen to reason."

Thereupon, one mandarin pulled Pan Tzu's sleeve to attract his attention, while the other whispered, "Do not betray us. Do not mention our names again, and we, too, will reward you. Just lead the Emperor to the well in the eastern courtyard. We have hidden the seal there."

Pan Tzu heard and understood. He nodded to the two thieves, and then he quite clearly said, "The seal is in the Royal Well, in the eastern courtyard."

And it was!

Overjoyed, the Emperor offered to reward Pan Tzu with 59

a high position at the Imperial Court. But the frightened Pan Tzu refused the offer. He wanted nothing but to get away from the palace. Then the poor fellow thought of what his wife would say if he came home empty-handed. "There is something I would like to have," he told the Emperor. "A blanket made of spun-sugar candy."

That was something his wife might like, he thought. She could nibble upon the sweet coverlet at night, and with her mouth full, she would not be able to nag him.

And so, though the Emperor thought the request was strange, a spun-sugar blanket was made.

But when Pan Tzu returned home with it, his wife flew into a rage. She had expected him to come back with bags of silver and strings of bright new *cash,* perhaps even with jewels and honors. And each day, she told him so.

Pan Tzu did not remain at home long. His next summons came from the Empress. She had heard how the jade seal had been recovered, and now she wanted to test Pan Tzu's remarkable powers of smell herself.

The Empress had a favorite maid, who was called Small Kitten because of her little pointed face and purring voice. Before Pan Tzu arrived, the Empress had Small Kitten put into a sack made of silk. The sack was placed inside a large chest, and the chest stuffed full of downy quilts. After the chest was closed, Pan Tzu was admitted to the royal quarters.

"Use your marvelous sense of smell to tell me what I have in this chest," said the Empress.

The chest seemed to waver and swim before Pan Tzu's eyes. He had no idea what was in it. His gaze darted to this door and that. All the doors were closed, and he knew that they were also well-guarded on the other side. He felt trapped, like a cat in a bag about to be drowned.

"The cat in the bag dies!" he cried desperately.

"How clever you are!" exclaimed the Empress. "There is a cat in that chest—my own little maid, Small Kitten! But I do not want her dead! Hurry, open the chest," she commanded her maids.

Indeed, when they lifted the quilts and tore open the sack, Small Kitten lay quite still, as though she were dead.

The other maids fanned Small Kitten's face and rubbed her hands. At long last, her eyes fluttered open, and she breathed once more.

"Pan Tzu," said the Empress, "you not only told me what was in the chest, but you also warned me that my little maid's life was in danger. Again you have proved your superhuman sense of smell. Truly, you are not an ordinary man. You must

61

be one of the gods. You do not belong on earth with mortal men. Your proper home is in the heavens." At these words, the strongest among the maids seized Pan Tzu, rushed him out into the Royal Gardens, and tossed him high up into the sky.

When at last he fell back to earth, Pan Tzu broke into millions of little pieces, which scattered all over the world. These little pieces turned into ants. And since that time, even from afar, ants find their way to good things to eat by using their remarkable sense of smell.

THREE ANECDOTES

Stealing the Bell

A man tried to steal a large bronze bell. It was too heavy to carry, so he tried to break up the valuable bronze with a hammer. But this made such a din that the thief feared he would be heard and discovered by the authorities. So he hastily stuffed his ears with cotton.

Only a fool would fool himself.

The Potter and the Gate

In a certain village, there was once a pottery-maker who was new to the business. One day, he tied his pots in two nets and fastened a net to each end of a bamboo pole. Then he lifted the pole to his back, hooked his arms over it, and set off to sell his pots in a nearby city.

When he reached the gate of the city, he found that he could not walk through it with his carrying pole across his back. The gate was too narrow.

He lifted the pole straight up. One bundle of pots banged on the ground, and the other bundle hit the top of the gate. He still could not get through. The gate was very low. So he stood there, wondering how to get into the city with his pole and his pots.

While he puzzled over the matter, another man arrived at the gate and observed the unhappy situation. "If I were you," said the newcomer, "I would go through the gate sideways."

"Of course" the potter exclaimed. "Why didn't I think of that myself?" And, holding his pole sideways, he entered the gate easily.

Often others can see a simple solution to the problem which puzzles us.

Marking the Boat to Locate the Sword

A man from the state of Chu was riding across the river on a ferry when his sword fell into the water. Immediately, the man put a scratch on the side of the boat.

"This is the exact spot from which my sword dropped into the water," he said.

When the ferry had been moored, the man jumped into the water to look for his sword under the spot he had marked on the boat. He dived down again and again, and he could not understand why he could not find his sword. After all, he had marked the spot so carefully.

He who marks the boat to
find the sword toils in vain.

THE MAN WHO
WOULD KNOW MAGIC

Wang Kai-Tse, seventh son of a prosperous family, longed to learn the Taoist religion and the secrets of Tao magic. When he heard that there were a number of Taoist priests at the monastery on Lao-Shan, he set off at once for the mountain.

At the monastery, Wang found an ancient priest with long flowing hair, sitting on a rush mat. Wang made a low, respectful bow, and the old priest looked up at him pleasantly.

"I long to learn the mysteries of Taoism," Wang said. "I am willing to work diligently. Will you teach me your secrets, Most Honorable Old One?"

"I fear it would be too much for you," the old priest replied. "I can see by your hands that you are not accustomed to work."

"Try me," Wang begged. "I will do anything you ask."

The priest agreed. "Tonight you will meet the eight other disciples at the monastery, and tomorrow, you will start to work, to humble your spirit."

Early the next morning, the priest sent Wang and the other pupils out to cut firewood.

For the next month, Wang did nothing but chop wood. Before long, his hands were blistered, his feet were swollen. Every muscle ached so that he could scarcely sleep. Secretly, he thought of going home.

One evening, when Wang and the other disciples returned from the woods, they found two strangers sitting at a table, drinking wine with the old priest. It was already dark; yet no candles had been lit. The old priest took a pair of scissors and cut out a circle of white paper. This he stuck on the wall.

At once, the circle became a dazzling moon that lit up the whole room. Curious, Wang and the disciples crowded into the room. "This is a festive occasion," their master said. "Let us all enjoy ourselves."

He took a small jug of wine from the table and handed it to the disciples, bidding each one to drink his fill.

Wang wondered how nine of them could get enough to drink out of a single jug. Nevertheless, to his amazement, after all had taken wine from the jug, it was still nearly full.

After a while, one of the strangers smiled at their master. "You have given us a fine, bright moon and provided us with wine," he said. "But we have had no entertainment. Why not call a Moon Lady to join us?" Even as the stranger spoke, the old priest threw a chopstick at the moon. Whereupon, a lovely girl stepped forth from its beams. At first, she was only a foot high, but as she came closer, she grew larger and larger, until she was the size of a woman. She had a slender waist and a beautiful neck, and she moved gracefully through the steps of an ancient dance. When the dance was finished, she smiled, jumped up on the table, and before the eyes of the astonished disciples, once more became a chopstick.

The old priest and his two friends laughed, and one of them said, "This is all very pleasant, but we must leave in a little while. Before we go, let us drink a parting glass of wine in the palace of the moon."

The three men stood up and walked into the moon, where the disciples could see them as plainly as reflections in a looking glass. By and by, the moon began to fade, and the room became dark again. When the disciples brought in lighted 69

candles they found the old priest sitting alone in the dark. The wine jug, however, was still on the table and the round piece of white paper was still on the wall.

Another ten days passed, and nothing exciting happened again. Since the old priest had taught him no magic tricks, Wang once more thought about returning home.

"I have been here for two months and have done nothing but chop firewood," he complained to the old priest. "Out in the morning and back at night. This is work to which I was never accustomed."

"Did I not tell you that you could not stand the work here?" said the priest. "Tomorrow I shall send you back home."

"But I have worked hard for you," Wang argued. "Surely in return, you can teach me a trifling magic trick. I crave to have some knowledge of your art."

"What do you long to learn?" the old priest asked.

"Well," answered Wang, "many times, I have noticed that whenever you walk about, walls are no obstacle to you. Teach me how to walk through walls and I'll be satisfied."

The priest laughingly agreed, and he taught Wang some magic words. He told Wang to recite these words first and then to walk through the monastary wall. Wang repeated the magic formula and walked slowly up to the wall. He stopped there, facing the solid brick.

The priest urged him on. "Don't go so slowly," the priest exclaimed. "Put your head down and rush at the wall."

Wang stepped back a few paces, then went at the wall full speed. The wall seemed to vanish before him and in a moment, he found himself outside. Delighted, Wang went back to thank his master. The old priest solemnly warned Wang never to show off his new skill, but to use it with great care.

When Wang returned to his family, he could not resist bragging about his Taoist friends and of his ability to walk through walls. His brothers did not believe him.

"I'll prove it to you!" Wang shouted, forgetting the solemn warning of the old priest. Stepping back from the garden wall, he put his head down and rushed forward at full speed. There was a dreadful crack, and Wang fell to the ground.

His brothers rushed to him and found he had a bump on his head as big as a duck's egg. At this, they roared with laughter. But Wang was overwhelmed with rage and shame. He cursed the old priest on Lao-Shan and all the Tao magic with him.

MA LIANG AND
HIS MAGIC BRUSH*

Ma Liang's parents died when he was still a small boy. He earned his living by gathering firewood, pulling weeds, and cutting rushes from the riverbank.

One day, the boy found work weeding the garden of a private school. There he saw the master showing his pupils how to paint. Liang was fascinated by the graceful strokes of the brush and the beauty of the master's picture. From that moment, the boy longed to paint, but of course he could not

---

*This version of a traditional tale is told in the Peoples Republic of China.

afford to buy a brush.

"Please, will you lend me a brush?" he asked the master softly. "I want so much to paint."

The master turned upon him angrily. "What! A beggar like you wants to paint? How dare you annoy me!" And he drove the boy away.

"Why shouldn't I learn to paint even though I am poor?" Liang said to himself. "Since I cannot buy a brush, I shall learn to draw some other way."

Thereafter, when he went up into the mountain to gather firewood, he looked for a patch of soft ground and drew birds and beasts in the dirt with the point of a stick. When he went to the river to cut reeds, he dipped his finger into the water and traced fish and turtles on the rocks.

People began to notice and marvel at his pictures. The birds he painted seemed about to fly, the fish to swim through the water, and the trees to sway in the breeze. But still, Ma Liang had no brush with which to make the soft, sweeping strokes he so loved in paintings.

One night, when Liang lay down on his hard pallet, a brush was the last thing he thought of before his eyes closed in sleep.

"Ma Liang," someone said. And an old man with a long

white beard appeared and put a brush in his hand.

"This is a magic brush," the Old One told the boy. "Use it carefully."

The boy awakened with a start. Alas, the magic brush was only a dream, he thought sadly. But no, there was the brush in his hand!

Instead of buying rice for the next three days, Ma Liang bought an ink stick and a sheet of paper. He painted a bird with his magic brush, and the bird flapped its wings and soared into the sky, singing. He painted a fish with his magic brush, and the fish frisked its tail and plunged into the river and swam about happily. People began to bring him sheets of paper to paint on. With his magic brush, Ma Liang painted for the poor folk in his village. He painted a plow for one, a hoe for another, an oil lamp for a venerable grandmother, and a stout water bucket for a mother who had none.

The news of Ma Liang's magic brush soon reached the ears of Li Ssu, a rich landlord in the village. The landlord sent two of his men to bring Ma Liang to him.

"From now on you will paint only for me," the landlord told Liang.

Even though the landlord threatened to have him beaten, Liang refused to paint a single picture for him. So the landlord shut Liang up in a stable, without food or water.

The weather turned bitter cold. Snow fell for three days and covered the ground thickly. Thinking that Ma Liang must have died of cold and hunger, Li Ssu went to the stable.

As he came near the door, he saw the glow of firelight and smelled delicious cooked food. Peeping through a crack, the landlord saw Ma Liang sitting comfortably by a big stove, eating roast duck! Li Ssu could not believe his eyes. Where had the stove and the roast duck come from? Then he remembered that Ma Liang could paint anything he needed. Trembling with rage, Li Ssu ordered his men to kill Ma Liang and to seize the magic brush.

When the landlord and a dozen of his strong men rushed into the stable, Ma Liang was nowhere to be seen. All they found was a ladder, leaning against the wall. The furious landlord leaped to the ladder. Before he had climbed three rungs, he fell down in a heap. When he scrambled to his feet, the ladder had vanished.

But Ma Liang's troubles were not over with his escape. He knew that he could not hide in the village, for the landlord would search every house. Whoever sheltered him would also be in trouble. The only thing to do was to go far away.

The boy made some strokes in the air with his magic

brush, and a fine, strong horse sprang to life. He mounted the steed and galloped down the highway.

He had not gone far when he heard the thunder of horses' hoofs behind him. The landlord and his men were riding hard after him. The cruel Li Ssu was shouting angrily and waving a sword.

Ma Liang painted a bow and an arrow in the air with his magic brush. Instantly the bow and arrow were in his hands, and the arrow was whizzing toward the landlord. It pierced his throat, and the landlord fell dead on the spot. Thus, Ma Liang got away safely.

He rode for several days and nights without stopping. When he came to a city, he decided to stay there and support himself by painting pictures. To make sure that his magic brush remained a secret, he never quite finished his pictures, so they never came to life. He drew birds without beaks or with unfinished wings and animals with a leg or a tail missing.

One day a villager asked Ma Liang to paint a crane. He painted the bird without eyes. As he was about to lay his brush down, someone jolted his arm and two drops of ink splashed onto the painting exactly where the crane's eyes should have been. The bird opened its eyes, flapped its wings and flew off the drawing paper.

The crowd around Ma Liang gasped and scattered to tell others about the marvel they had seen. Soon, the Emperor learned of it and sent officers to bring the young artist to him.

Ma Liang had heard many stories of how cruel the Emperor was to the poor. He resolved never to serve such a man.

So, when the Emperor ordered him to paint a golden dragon, Ma Liang painted a green toad. When the Emperor wanted a scarlet phoenix, Ma Liang produced a brown rooster. The toad and the rooster hopped and flapped about the palace, making a terrible racket and breaking all sorts of precious ornaments. No one could catch them.

In a rage, the Emperor ordered his guards to seize the magic brush and then throw Ma Liang into the darkest prison.

The Emperor lost no time in making use of the magic brush. He painted a golden mountain, decided one was not enough and added another and another. When the painting was finished, instead of turning into real mountains of gold, they changed into ordinary rocks which crashed onto the palace floor.

The greedy Emperor thought he had made a mistake somewhere. So this time he painted a gold brick. It seemed too small, so he painted it bigger and bigger and bigger. When at last he had finished, the painting came to life, not as an enormous gold brick, but as a huge yellow serpent. The serpent wrapped itself around the Emperor and would have crushed him to death, but the palace guards rushed in with their swords and cut the monster to pieces.

Since the Emperor could not make use of the magic brush himself, he ordered Ma Liang brought to him. This time, the Emperor spoke kindly, gave Liang gold and silver, and even promised him a princess in marriage. Ma Liang was not fooled. He knew that imperial promises were worthless. He had already made a plan while in prison, and now he began to carry it out. He agreed to everything the Emperor wanted, so the magic brush was given back to him.

The Emperor was very pleased, but he did not trust Ma Liang entirely. "If I ask him to paint a beast," he thought, "the creature may come to life and devour me. I had better ask him to paint the sea." And so he did.

Ma Liang took up his magic brush, stroked the air with it, and soon he was able to show the Emperor a calm and boundless sea.

"There are no fish in that sea," the Emperor remarked. "Why is that?"

Ma Liang made a few dabs with his magic brush, and
the sea was filled with fish that glittered like jewels. The fish

frisked about, then turned and swam slowly toward the horizon.

The Emperor watched the fish with delight. Perhaps they really were jewels. He wanted to catch one and see. "Quickly, paint a boat!" he commanded Liang. "I want to go after those marvelous fish."

Ma Liang painted a large boat, with a magnificent sail. The Emperor called to his ministers, and they all went aboard. A light breeze filled the sail, and the boat moved gracefully out to sea.

It was too slow for the Emperor. "Let the wind blow harder!" he shouted. "Harder!"

A few strokes of the magic brush, and a strong wind whistled after the boat. Whitecaps ruffled the sea, and the boat sail billowed. Ma Liang drew a few more strokes in the air. The wind roared, the sea rose, and the boat began to rock dangerously.

"That's enough wind!" shouted the Emperor. "Enough, I say!"

Ma Liang paid no attention. He continued to wave his brush in the air, painting a still-rougher sea with a still-higher wind. Billowing waves washed over the ship.

The Emperor clung to the mast, shaking his fist and

shouting at Ma Liang.

The young artist pretended to hear nothing and went on drawing waves and wind. Soon he had a hurricane blowing, with huge waves rising higher and higher and crashing onto the boat. At last, the vessel broke into pieces. The Emperor and his ministers sank to the bottom of the sea.

After the Emperor's death, the story of Ma Liang and his magic brush spread far and wide. But what became of Ma Liang and his magic brush? Nobody knows for certain. Some say he went back to his native village and his peasant friends. Others say that he roamed all over China, painting for the poor wherever he went.

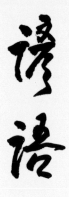

IN CHINA
THE PEOPLE SAY...

Short sayings based on long experience

When wings are grown, birds and children fly away.

He who rides in a chair is a man. It is well to remember that those who carry the chair are also men.

Water and words are easy to pour, but impossible to recover.

The home which has an old grandparent in it contains a precious jewel.

Looking for fish? Do not climb a tree.

O eggs, never fight with stones!

The wise man listens to his own mind, the foolish man heeds
the mob.

A teacher can open the door, but the pupil must go through
by himself.

Every day cannot be a Feast of Lanterns.

The stream far away cannot extinguish the fires nearby.

Patience and the mulberry leaf become a silk gown.

Talk does not cook rice.

To forget one's ancestors is to be a brook without a source, a
tree without roots.

All the flowers of all the tomorrows are in the seeds of today.   *85*

ABOUT THIS BOOK...

Notes and Sources

China has more than three thousand years of recorded history, and it has myths, legends, folktales, and anecdotes without number, dating from ancient times. This collection was culled from many sources and interpreted to preserve the original spirit of the tales, the oral quality of wayside storytellers, and the coziness of anecdotes told and retold on quiet evenings.

A variety of subject matter and a cross section of society is represented: customs, religions, ideas and ideals of virtue, duty, filial piety, industry, studiousness, honesty and dishonesty, thrift and greed, politeness, wisdom and foolishness, and lively nonsense.

Themes from folklore have always inspired the art of a nation, and it is just so in China. These stories and explanatory notes will help the reader recognize some of the characters painted on plates, trays, teacups, scrolls, and vases or carved in ivory and jade: the Eight Immortals, the phoenix, the crane, the unicorn, and other symbols from myths.

Discovery of Salt. The mythical phoenix (*feng-huang*) of this story is as much a legend in China as *Ki-lin,* the gentle unicorn. This fabulous bird is supposed to have had an amiable nature, nobility, and wisdom. Even in ancient times, the bird was supposed to have appeared rarely. When it did, it perched over hidden treasure, on which fortunate circumstance this story is hung.

The phoenix is like a peacock, with a small head and body and a long, brilliantly feathered tail. The head, breast, and back are scarlet, the wings feathered in iridescent colors, the eyes sea-blue. The phoenix is very popular as a decoration in Chinese art. It was the emblem of Chinese empresses, just as the dragon was the emblem of the emperors.

The Wise Man's Pillow. This tale is based on *Chen Chung Chi,* (*Record of the Inside of a Pillow*), by Shen Chi-chih, *circa* A.D.780.

The Eight Immortals are Taoist gods. They frequently visited earth, and their visits often affected the lives of mortals. So it may well be that the Taoist priest featured in this story was one of the remarkable Eight.

The Marvelous Pear Seed. The phrase "clean wind in his sleeves" means that the person or official is honest.

The Young Head of the Cheng Family and *Legend of How Ants Came to Earth.* These tales were selected, and adapted especially for this book, from the forty stories in Adele Fielde's *Chinese Nights' Entertainments* (published in 1893), which the author collected during her residence in Kwantung Province in southern China. The stories emerge from the romance of *The Strayed Arrow,* in which each tale is told either by the boys' schoolmaster or by one of his pupils. As a change of pace from schoolwork, the boys insisted that the stories be "without a moral" and be told just for fun. And so emerges an amusing string of typical Chinese tales, with each story like a bead on the string—all drawn to a conclusion in an Oriental climax.

Gift of the Unicorn. This tale is the legendary story of Confucius' birth. The Chinese unicorn is a popular omen of good. Chinese people say that Confucius was "the elf of the unicorn." An extraordinarily bright boy is often referred to as the "son of the unicorn" or "gift of the unicorn." At the Feast of Lanterns, in the middle of the first month of the Chinese New Year, vendors sell a lantern that represents a boy riding a unicorn. When someone purchases such a lantern and gives it to a friend, he means: "I wish that you may have a very bright son."

In his writings, Confucius presented a code of ethics, or rules for behavior in public as well as private life. He believed these rules would enable the people of China to live more happily.

The Man Who Stole a Rope. This anecdote crops up in various collections of Chinese literature and humor, and it is frequently told orally. The wearing of the cangue was listed among the legal modes of Chinese punishment and torture. The cangue, a wooden collar, was fastened around the neck of the victim, and he was then placed on public display during the daytime. His crime and length of punishment were inscribed on the upper side of the cangue. The size of the collar prevented the victim from being able to reach his mouth with his hands, so he had to depend on kind passersby or friends to put food in his mouth. At night, he was taken back to jail by the constable, and the collar was removed. This punishment sometimes lasted for as long as three months.

The Borrowing of 100,000 Arrows. This incident has been extracted and adapted from Chapter 46 of *San Kuo Yen Yi*, (*Romance of the Three Kingdoms*), one of China's most popular novels, which is attributed to Lo Kuan-chung, also known as Lo Pen, a native of Hangchow (*circa* 1364). The action of this historical novel takes place at the beginning of the third century A.D. This period was one of confusion, with the three kingdoms of Wei, Shu, and Wu almost constantly at war for supremacy.

The Man Who Sold a Ghost. This tale is based on a story in *Lieh Yi Chuan*, or *Strange Tales*. The authorship is uncertain, but they were probably written before the year 300 A.D. Stories debunking demons, gods, magic, and witches are also popular today.

A Warning from the Gods. Had the people of Ta-yeh listened to the good Niang-tzu, she would have gone down in legend as a lady Noah. Since they did not, they perished, and she became part of the story of the creation of Liang-ti Lake and had an island named in her honor.

The Potter and the Gate. This version is based on a fragment of an anecdote from *Hsiao Lin*, (*The Forest of Smiles*), which was compiled by Han-tan Shun in about the third century. Although the original work is now lost, some twenty anecdotes or fragments from it are to be found in later works.

Stealing the Bell and *Marking the Boat to Locate the Sword* have similar characters and action, which make this group of tales comparable to the stories of amiable blockheads and their adventures in the noodle or noddy tales of other lands.

The Man Who Would Know Magic. Taoism was one of the three main religions of old China, the others being Confucianism and Buddhism. *Tao* means *The*

Way, and it was founded by the sage Lao Tze as a philosophy and a guide by which man could attain happiness. Later, Taoists began to practice magic, believe in spirits, superstitions, and the supernatural.

Ma Liang and His Magic Brush. In present-day China, many traditional myths, folktales, fables, and anecdotes have been completely rewritten, and others have been changed to promote the Communist ideology of the Peking government. Especially favored are stories which portray high officials, emperors, princes, judges, or landlords as cruel, wicked, dishonest, stupid or ridiculous. Peasants are wise, good, helpful, warm-hearted, resourceful, and brave. In the story of Ma Liang, all these features are particularly evident.

This type of propaganda is not new. Stories and fables told for entertainment have always had another purpose: the teaching of a lesson by means of the point made in the story. Many of these stories had a basis in fact. They were one way in which the people could tell their leaders how *they* felt without losing their heads. Political figures also used fables and anecdotes to make a point and to add pith to their pitch. The propaganda possibilities of national folklore were eagerly seized upon by the Communists in both Russia and, later, in China, and now these tales are presented as ancient "people wisdom." The fact that they have been rewritten to fit a particular ideology is carefully omitted.

ACKNOWLEDGMENTS

I would like to acknowledge my debt to the writers and translators whose scholarship and works were most helpful in interpreting the contents of this book: the Reverend Justus Doolittle, *Social Life and Customs of the Chinese*, 2 vols., (Harper & Bros., 1865); Professor Herbert Allen Giles, *Strange Stories from a Chinese Studio*, taken from *Liao-chai chih-i*, by P'u Sung-ling [*circa* 1640-1715], (Kelly & Walsh, Shanghai, 1880); also Professor Giles, *History of Chinese Literature*, originally published in 1901, (Frederick Unger Publishing Co., New York, 1967); and Professor Giles' *Chinese Fairy Tales*, (Gowans and Gray, 1911); Adele M. Fielde, *Chinese Fairy Tales*, (G. P. Putnam's Sons, 1893); also her *Chinese Nights Entertainments*, (G. P. Putnam's Sons, 1893); E. T. C. Werner, *Myths and Legends of China*, (George Harrap, London, 1922; Farrar & Rinehart, New York, 1922); also his *A Dictionary of Chinese Mythology*, originally published by Kelly & Walsh, Shanghai, 1932, (Julian Press, New York, 1961); Ch'en Shou-Yi, *Chinese Literature: a Historical Introduction*, (Ronald Press, New York, 1961); Ch'u Chai and Winberg Chai, *A Treasury of Chinese Literature*. (Appleton-Century, New York, 1965); Wolfram Eberhard, ed., *Folktales of China*, (E. P. Dutton, New York, 1938; University of Chicago Press, Chicago, 1965); Gertrude Jacobs, *Chinese-American Song and Game Book*, (A. S. Barnes & Co., Inc., Cranbury, New Jersey, 1944); Anthony Christie, *Chinese Mythology*, (Paul Hamlyn, Feltham, England, 1968); R. de Rohan Barondes, *China: Lore, Legend and Lyrics*, (Philosophical Library, New York, 1960); Mary Hayes Davis and Chow-Leung, *Chinese Fables and Folk Stories*, (American Book Co., New York, 1908); Dennis Bloodworth, *The Chinese Looking Glass*, (Farrar, Straus & Giroux, New York, 1966); Gladys Yang and Yang Hsien-Yi, *Ancient Chinese Fables*, (Foreign Language Press, Peking, 1957); *Folk Tales from China* [compiler unlisted], (Foreign Language Press, Peking, 1957); Chi-Chen Wang, translator of *Dream of the Red Chamber,* by Ts'ao Hsueh-Chin, published in 1792, (Twayne, New York, 1958; Doubleday Anchor Books, New York, 1958).

My thanks must also be extended to Dr. Francis Paar of the Oriental Room in the New York Public Library; to Mrs. Dorothea Creamer, Circulation Librarian, and Mr. Silvio Lam, Reference Librarian at Friendship Library, Fairleigh Dickinson University; and to my wife, Lee Wyndham, who helped me sieve out the nuggets for this collection from a vast quantity of material.

—ROBERT WYNDHAM
Morristown, New Jersey

Books by ROBERT WYNDHAM

TALES THE PEOPLE TELL IN CHINA

CHINESE MOTHER GOOSE RHYMES

THE LITTLE WISE MAN (with Lee Wyndham)